SPORTS FROM COAST TO COAST™

BASKETBALL
RULES, TIPS, STRATEGY, AND SAFETY

— FRED RAMEN —

rosen publishing's
rosen central®

New York

Published in 2007 by The Rosen Publishing Group, Inc.
29 East 21st Street, New York, NY 10010

First Edition

Library of Congress Cataloging-in-Publication Data

Ramen, Fred.
Basketball: rules, tips, strategy, and safety/Fred Ramen.—1st ed.
   p. cm.—(Sports from coast to coast)
Includes bibliographical references and index.
ISBN-13: 978-1-4042-0992-3
ISBN-10: 1-4042-0992-1 (library binding)
1. Basketball—Juvenile literature. I. Title. II. Series.

GV885.1.R36 2006
796.323—dc22

                                                    2006016128

Printed in China

CONTENTS

CHAPTER ONE

History of an American Game

Basketball was invented by Dr. James Naismith (*above*). He never suspected that one day it would be played around the world.

Basketball is a truly American sport. Unlike many other major sports, basketball did not evolve from other games or have an origin shrouded in myths and legends. It was invented by a single person in 1891, and since then it has become popular throughout the world.

People of both sexes and of all ages play pickup games in backyards, at gyms, and at playgrounds around the globe. College and university teams vie for championships every year. In addition, countries in North and South America, Europe, Asia, Africa, and Australia have their own professional men's leagues. Some of the best players from around the world now play in North America's National Basketball Association (NBA), including Tony Parker of France and Yao Ming of China.

Basketball's popularity is easy to understand. In the first place, it doesn't require a lot of equipment—just a hoop, a ball, and a flat, hard surface. In addition, the sport emphasizes agility and conditioning over physical strength, so anyone can play. You don't even have to be tall: Muggsy Bogues, who played for several NBA teams in the 1980s and 1990s, stood five feet three inches (1.6 meters) tall.

Basketball is a fun activity for you and your friends, and it's also a great way to improve your conditioning and coordination. It's no surprise so many people play this great American game.

Basketball's Inventor: James Naismith

Basketball was invented in America and first played by Americans, but the sport had an international flavor from the beginning. That's because the man who invented it was Canadian.

In 1891, James Naismith was a young teacher at the YMCA Training School in Springfield, Massachusetts. The school's physical education department wanted to develop a game that would be fun to play indoors, when the snow and cold made it impossible to send the young men outside. Naismith toyed with the idea of creating an indoor version of soccer or football, but he decided it would be too rough for a confined space. Instead, he invented his own game, developing thirteen simple rules for play. Players had to shoot a large ball into a basket high off the floor. They could not run with the ball, and they were not allowed to tackle or interfere with the person who held the ball.

Naismith chose an elevated target so that shooting at it would require the players to develop good hand-eye coordination. And by keeping players

The Thirteen Original Rules of Basketball

Here are James Naismith's original basketball rules. According to legend, he came up with the rules in about an hour. Most of them are still in effect in modified form today.

1. The ball may be thrown in any direction with one or both hands.
2. The ball may be batted in any direction with one or both hands.
3. A player cannot run with the ball. The player must throw it from the spot on which he catches it, allowances to be made for a man who catches the ball when running if he tries to stop.
4. The ball must be held by the hands. The arms or body must not be used for holding it.
5. No shouldering, holding, pushing, tripping, or striking in any way the person of an opponent shall be allowed; the first infringement of this rule by any player shall come as a foul, the second shall disqualify him until the next goal is made, or, if there was evident intent to injure the person, for the whole of the game, no substitute allowed.
6. A foul is striking the ball with the fist, violation of Rules 3, 4, and such as described in Rule 5.
7. If either side makes three consecutive fouls it shall count as a goal for the opponents (consecutive means without the opponents in the meantime making a foul).
8. A goal shall be made when the ball is thrown or batted from the grounds into the basket and stays there, providing those defending the goal do no touch or disturb the goal. If the ball rests on the edges, and the opponent moves the basket, it shall count as a goal.
9. When the ball goes out of bounds, it shall be thrown into the field of play by the person touching it. He has a right to hold it unmolested for five seconds. In case of a dispute, the umpire shall throw it straight into the field. The thrower-in is allowed five seconds; if he holds it longer it shall go to the opponent. If any side persists in delaying the game the umpire shall call a foul on that side.

10. The umpire shall be the judge of the men and shall note the fouls and notify the referee when three consecutive fouls have been made. He shall have power to disqualify men according to Rule 5.
11. The referee shall be judge of the ball and shall decide when the ball is in play, in bounds, to which side it belongs, and shall keep the time. He shall decide when a goal has been made and keep account of the goals, with any other duties that are usually performed by a referee.
12. The time shall be two fifteen-minute halves, with five minutes rest between.
13. The side making the most goals in that time shall be declared the winner. In the case of a draw the game may, by agreement of the captains, be continued until another goal is made.

from tackling the person with the ball, he achieved his goal of creating a game that rewarded quickness and agility over brute force.

The first-ever basketball game took place on December 21, 1891. It ended with a score of 1–0. (Back then, baskets counted for only one point.) Naismith wanted to use a box as the goal, but the custodian could only find a peach basket, which he nailed to the wall. When the basket was scored, the custodian had to use a stepladder to retrieve the ball. Soon, Naismith decided to cut the bottom out of the basket to speed up play.

Basketball Gains in Popularity

Naismith's new game spread rapidly. The first game between high school teams was played in 1897, and colleges soon got into the act, too. By the 1930s, several tournaments were being held between the best college teams in the country. Two of these tournaments, the National Collegiate Athletic Association (NCAA) tournament and the National Invitational Tournament (NIT), are still played today. The NCAA tournament is known as March Madness because most of the games are played in March and the students from rival schools provide a loud and raucous audience for the games.

This photograph shows an early high school basketball game. Notice that the net is closed at the bottom. After every basket, someone had to climb up to retrieve the ball.

Professional basketball began soon after the invention of the game, but organized leagues took a while to catch on. During the 1920s and 1930s, many independent pro teams went on "barnstorming" tours, playing in different towns against all comers. Attempts were made to start a nationwide professional league, but none really caught on. Finally, two pro leagues merged to form the National Basketball Association (NBA).

The NBA played its first season in 1949–1950. For the first few years, the NBA games regularly ended with teams failing to score sixty points. League officials thought of ways to make the game more exciting, so in the 1954–1955 season, the NBA introduced the shot clock. This innovation completely altered the way basketball is played. Since then, it has been a part of organized basketball at all levels. The shot clock requires that the team with the ball take a shot within twenty-four seconds (in the NBA) or thirty-five seconds (in college and high school ball). This rule greatly increased offense and led to the fast-paced game so popular with spectators today.

Rule changes have an impact on the game, but it is the talented players who make basketball fun to watch. In the 1960s, the great Boston Celtics won eight consecutive NBA championships. Wilt Chamberlain was the most dominant individual player of the era, but the Celtics played superior team basketball. Later, in the 1980s, two players changed the face of basketball

Bob Cousy of the Boston Celtics (*left*) drives to the basket. In winning eight consecutive NBA titles, Cousy and the Celtics showed that teamwork beats individual talent in basketball.

again. When Ervin "Magic" Johnson and Larry Bird arrived on the scene, they proved that big players could handle the ball and be great passers and shooters, too. As Johnson and Bird approached retirement, Michael Jordan emerged as the most popular NBA player ever. He led the Chicago Bulls to six championships in the 1990s and helped spread the game to the far corners of the globe.

Today's brightest NBA stars include LeBron James, Kobe Bryant, and Steve Nash. These players join the long list of greats who have made Naismith's simple game so entertaining.

CHAPTER TWO

Who's Who on the Court

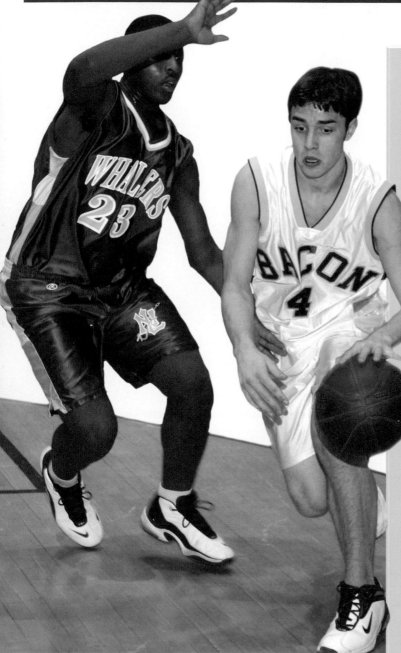

A player drives past his defender on the way to the basket. Individual matchups like this provide a big part of the excitement in basketball.

Basketball can be played almost anywhere you have a flat surface and a place to hang a hoop. In addition, the game rules can be altered to fit the circumstances. The following two chapters focus on regulation play, the way basketball is played in high school, college, and the NBA.

Basic Strategy

The objective in basketball is very simple: to score more field goals—the official term for baskets—than the other team. The offense, or the team in possession of the ball, tries to take a good shot before the shot clock expires. To do this, they run set plays. They pass the ball, move around the court, and use tactics such as screens and picks to get the ball to a player with an open shot at the basket.

For its part, the defense counters with strategies to prevent the offense from getting a good shot. In individual matchups, a defensive player will position his or her body between the basket and the player with the ball. The defender may also try to take the ball away from the ball handler (a tactic called a steal). Defenses also run their own plays as a team. For example, a defense may double-team or trap an offensive player. This involves putting two defenders on the player with the ball to prevent an easy pass or shot. More detailed defensive plays are discussed in chapter 3.

The Court

The regulation basketball court for the NBA and college levels is a rectangle and is fifty feet wide by ninety-four feet (15.2 m by 28.7 m) long. Most high school courts are eighty-four feet (25.6 m) long. The hoops, or rims, are located at either end of the court. They are suspended ten feet (3 m) off the ground and are attached to backboards that measure six feet (1.8 m) across. The backboards are hung so that they are four feet (1.2 m) in from the baseline.

Several lines are painted on the court. The outside lines are considered out-of-bounds. If a player with the ball steps on a boundary line, or if the ball touches it, the referee whistles the play dead. The division line, or midcourt line, separates the backcourt from the frontcourt. After a made basket, the offense must take the ball out-of-bounds and then pass it in, bringing it into the frontcourt within a certain amount of time—eight seconds in the NBA. Failure to do so means they turn the ball over to the other team. A circle with

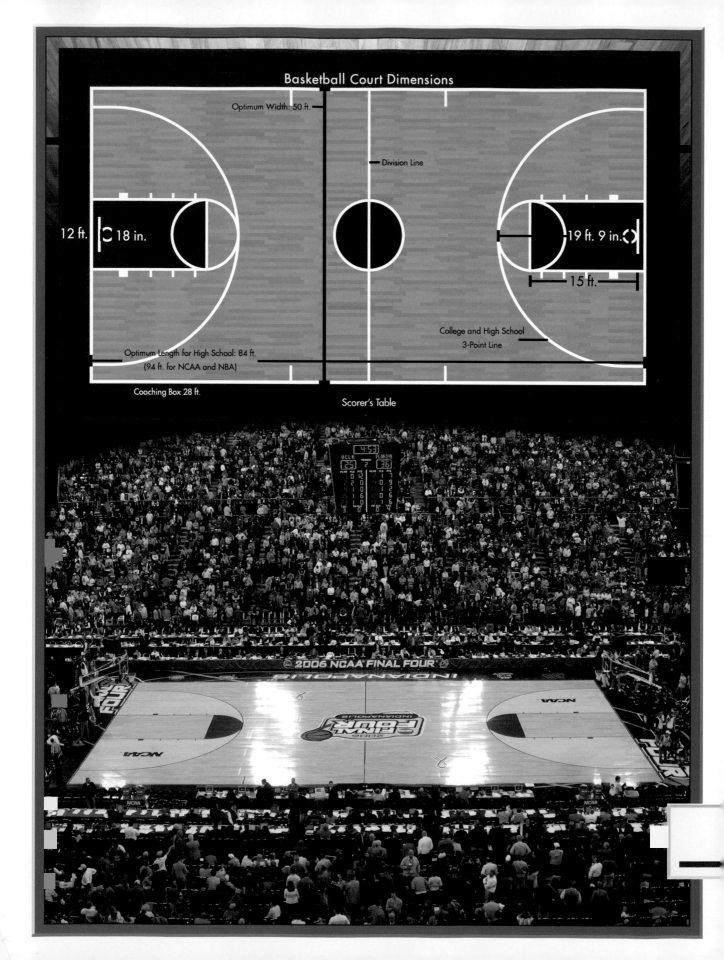

Basketball Court Dimensions

Optimum Width: 50 ft.

Division Line

12 ft.   18 in.

19 ft. 9 in.

15 ft.

College and High School
3-Point Line

Optimum Length for High School: 84 ft.
(94 ft. for NCAA and NBA)

Coaching Box 28 ft.

Scorer's Table

a six-foot (1.8 m) radius is painted at the center of the midcourt line. This circle is where the opening tip-off, or jump ball, takes place.

A foul line, or free throw line, is located fifteen feet (4.6 m) from each backboard. Free throws—special shots awarded for getting fouled—must be taken from behind this line. Each foul line marks the diameter of a circle that may also be used for jump balls. A rectangular area underneath each basket is called the free throw lane, or lane. This is where players line up when a foul shot is being taken. Originally, the free throw lane was narrower, and in combination with the circle around the free throw line, it looked like a keyhole. To this day, the point on the circle farthest from the basket is called the top of the key.

If an offensive player has even one foot in the free throw lane, he or she must take a shot within three seconds. The lane and the three-second rule prevent taller, stronger players from setting up close to the basket and taking very easy shots.

The three-point line is an arc that runs from the baseline to behind the top of the key. Shots made from behind this line count for three points instead of two. The NBA three-point line is farther away from the basket than the college and high school line.

The Positions

Five players from each team are allowed on the court at once. Each player has a special role in the team's defensive and offensive schemes. Typically, teams play with two guards, two forwards, and one center. However, a team may play with three guards, or three forwards, or even two centers. For convenience when designing plays, player positions are often numbered, one through five.

This diagram (*facing page, top*) shows a court laid out for a college or high school game. At bottom, the crowd awaits action in the 2006 NCAA championship tournament.

Guards

The point guard, or one-guard, is the field general for a basketball team. The point guard runs the offensive plays, so he or she needs to bounce—or dribble—the ball well. Good point guards dribble with their head up so they know where all the other players are at all times.

Just as important as dribbling is the ability to make good passes. The point guard must deliver the ball accurately so that teammates can catch the ball and shoot quickly. Accurate passes also prevent the other team from stealing the ball. Passing is so important to the game that if a pass leads directly to a score, the player who made the pass gets an assist. A high number of assists in a game indicates that the point guard is doing a good job.

Dribbling skills are important for all players but especially for guards. They handle the ball in the open court more than other players.

When the other team has the ball, the point guard is often the first line of defense. He or she will usually guard the other team's primary ball handler.

Many consider Michael Jordan the greatest all-around basketball player ever. He played shooting guard throughout his career but had the skills to play point guard, too.

When defending, the point guard tries to anticipate the other team's plays, stealing the ball when the opportunity presents itself.

Point guards are often the shortest players on the team. Being closer to the ground, a shorter point guard does not have to bounce the ball as high, which increases ball control. A taller point guard has the advantage of being able to see over a defender, making it easier to make a pass. One of the keys to Magic Johnson's success as a point guard was the fact that he stood 6 feet 9 inches (2.06 m) tall.

A good shooting guard is a threat to score from just about any spot on the court. Here, a shooting guard launches an outside jump shot.

The team's other guard, sometimes called the two-guard or shooting guard, is typically a good scorer. Usually, this means he or she is an accurate outside shooter. However, some two-guards are only mediocre shooters who score by penetrating, or getting close to the basket, using their speed and ball-handling skills.

The best two-guards can move in any direction, releasing shots from any spot on the court. Michael Jordan, who was a two-guard, became one of the game's top scorers because he was both a great shooter and a great ball handler. He was also very creative and original with his moves, which made him even more difficult to defend.

Two-guards are usually bigger than point guards, but they tend to be smaller than the forwards or centers, so they aren't expected to rebound much.

"She Got Game": Basketball Expressions

Like athletes in other sports, basketball players have their own specialized words, or lingo. If you want to sound like a "gym rat" (see below), use some of these expressions:

air ball A missed field goal attempt that fails to touch the rim or the backboard.

alley-oop A pass thrown high in the air above the basket so that another player can slam-dunk it.

boards The backboards. Also, rebounds: "He had ten boards in that game."

game Good basketball skills, as in, "She got game."

gym rat A player who is always practicing basketball, often alone. Real gym rats are the first ones to arrive at practice and the last ones to leave.

run To play basketball. On the playground, people might ask you if you "want to run" with them, meaning play basketball with them.

stick the J Make a jump shot. "You can dribble, but can you stick the J?"

stuff To dunk the ball. Also, to block a shot: "He went in for a layup and got stuffed."

we've got next In playground basketball, the team that wins gets to stay on the court. If you want to play the winners, say, "We've got next," to stake your claim.

zebras The referees; at most levels they wear black and white striped shirts.

For a game of one-on-one, these gym rats play without zebras.

When playing under the basket, forwards can expect body contact every time they shoot.

Forwards

Guards play away from the basket, but forwards play close to the basket, often just under it. They are generally taller and bigger than guards. At higher levels, players at this position are categorized as small forwards or power forwards. Small forwards, who play what is called the three position, are expected to score. On the other hand, power forwards, who play in the four position, are expected to rebound and play tough defense.

Forwards are generally not as good as guards at handling the ball. In addition, since they play closer to the basket, they don't have to have great outside shots.

Center

In the middle of the team's offense and defense is the center, who plays the five position. Centers are generally the biggest and tallest players on the court. They must provide strong defense against the other team's biggest player, while also preventing opposing guards

Shaquille O'Neal *(facing page, right)* is one of the best centers in NBA history. Here, he shoves his way to the basket to take a jump shot.

and forwards from penetrating for easy shots. Good centers can block opponents' shots, and they are good rebounders, too. After pulling down a defensive rebound, a center usually looks to pass the ball immediately to a guard heading up the court.

It is not crucial for the center to be a good offensive player, but the better teams often have a center who is a good scorer. A center who can pass as well as score is a great advantage. Defensive teams often double-team a high-scoring center with the ball. So, a center who is adept at passing to an unguarded teammate can really help a team's offense. Because of their position, centers usually take most of their shots standing close to the basket.

Great centers such as Wilt Chamberlain, Bill Russell, Kareem Abdul-Jabbar, and Shaquille O'Neal have long dominated the pro game.

Coaches

The head coach of a team is responsible for creating the lineups, calling the plays on both offense and defense, and handling the substitutions during the game. Many head coaches, even at the lower levels, are aided by assistant coaches. During daily practices, coaches run exercises and drills for the players. A good coach is also a teacher who is constantly using his or her experience to help players improve their games.

Coaches make adjustments throughout the game. This head coach is diagramming a play for his team.

During the game, a coach will tell the team which plays to run using hand signals or code numbers. For offensive plays, coaches always try to take advantage of any weakness in the other team's defense. This could be a mismatch such as a short player guarding a tall one or a slow player guarding a quick one. For defense, coaches change their team's defensive setup depending on the strengths of the opposing team and the plays they run. Coaches also decide when to call time-outs to go over strategy or give players a needed rest.

CHAPTER THREE

Playing the Game

There have been many additions made to the rules of basketball since the first game was played. But the general principles of the game have remained unchanged. As in Naismith's day, the objective of the game is still to put the ball in the basket.

Getting the Game Under Way

Basketball games are made up of four quarters of play. In the NBA, each quarter is twelve minutes long. Depending on the league, college and high school games are made up of two twenty-minute halves or four ten-minute quarters. If the game is tied at the end of regulation time, a five-minute overtime period is played.

The first quarter begins with a tip-off, or jump ball. Two players, one from each team, stand in the

A player soars high to slam home the ball. The slam dunk is one of the most exciting plays in sports.

center circle at midcourt, with the other players gathered around them. No other players may enter the circle. When the referee throws the ball high in the air, the two players try to knock it to a teammate. Referees may also call for a jump ball at other times during the game, as when they are unable to determine which team knocked the ball out-of-bounds.

In college and high school, officials use the alternate-possession rule after the opening tip-off. This means that the team that does not take possession

The referee tosses the ball up for the opening tip-off, and the game is under way.

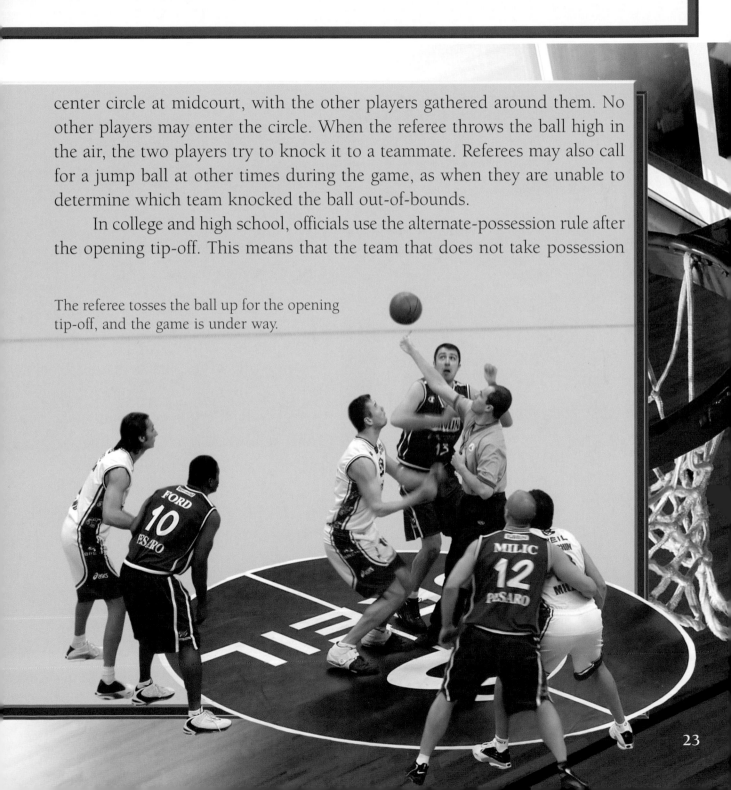

of the opening tip will be awarded possession of the ball if there is a held ball (two players from different teams each have possession) or at the beginning of the next quarter. Possession then alternates for the rest of the game. The alternate-possession rule was not always in effect. In the past, there would be a jump ball after each held ball. However, this slowed down the game, so the alternate-possession rule was created.

It is against the rules to make contact with the arm of an offensive player in the act of shooting. This defender *(right)* is clearly fouling the shooter.

That's a Foul!

When a player breaks the rules, the official calls a foul. One of the most common types of fouls is a shooting foul. These occur when a defensive player makes illegal contact with an opponent who is attempting a field goal. Following shooting fouls, a shooter is awarded two uncontested shots (or free throws) from behind the free throw line. Each made free throw counts as one point. If a player was attempting a field goal from behind the three-point line, he or she is awarded three free throws.

For non-shooting fouls, such as reaching in or holding, the offensive player is not usually awarded a free throw. Instead, the team whose player was fouled takes the ball out-of-bounds. However, after a team commits a certain number of fouls in a half, free throws are awarded for all fouls, shooting and non-shooting.

Common Fouls

charging An offensive foul called when a player runs into a defender who has established position.

elbowing Making contact with your elbows in an attempt to move or push away the other player.

flagrant foul Called for excessive or unnecessary contact.

holding Grabbing or otherwise preventing a player from moving freely.

loose ball foul A foul that occurs when neither team has possession, such as during a rebound.

over-the-back A foul called when a player makes contact while reaching over from behind a player in position to rebound.

reaching in Making illegal contact with the ball handler when trying to go for a steal.

technical foul Any action the referee believes is detrimental to the game. Technical fouls can be given to anybody on the team, not just the players on the court; even coaches can get technical fouls. A technical foul results in the other team getting one free throw and possession of the ball.

There is often a lot of contact on plays near the basket. It's up to the referee to decide if a foul is committed.

Offensive players commit fouls, too. They sometimes illegally charge into a defender while shooting or unfairly prevent a defender from getting into position. When an offensive foul is called, possession of the ball is awarded to the defending team. In most cases, offensive fouls do not result in free throws.

Players may not commit an unlimited number of fouls. In the NBA, a player is disqualified after committing six fouls, whether offensive or defensive. In lower-level games, players are disqualified after committing a fifth foul. A disqualified player may be replaced by another player, but he or she is not allowed to reenter the game.

Handling the Ball

In Naismith's original vision of the game, a player had to pass the ball right away. But the game evolved two rules to allow players to move around the court with the ball: the pivot and the dribble.

Pivoting in the Post

Pivots are an important part of every player's moves, especially centers. When you post up, or play with your back to the hoop, a good pivot move will allow you to move toward the basket and use your height to get off a good shot. Posting up requires you to use size and strength to force your defender out of position.

An important component in a good post move is the ability to fake. For this, you pretend to take a shot to get the defender to change position. Then, you pivot and spin to change the direction of the play. This creates distance between you and the defender, allowing for an easier shot. Because of their creative post-up moves, center Hakeem Olajuwon of the Houston Rockets and forward Kevin McHale of the Boston Celtics were practically unstoppable.

A player with the ball may pivot, or turn on one foot, in any direction without having to pass the ball. Once a player establishes a pivot foot, he or she cannot then pivot on the other foot. Switching pivots is a violation called traveling, which results in a turnover, meaning the other team takes possession of the ball.

A player is allowed to take one step with the ball. If you want to take more than one step with the ball, you must dribble it, or bounce it on the floor. Since you are not actually carrying the ball, moving while dribbling is not considered a traveling violation. There is no limitation on how high you can dribble the ball. You can use either hand to dribble, and even switch hands, but you cannot use both hands at the same time. This violation, called double-dribbling, is also a turnover.

Palming or carrying the ball is another ball-handling violation. A ball handler may not place the palm of his or her hand under the ball while dribbling. If the ball comes to rest in the dribbler's hand, the dribble has ended. Bouncing the ball again after it has come to rest is a violation.

Good shooters "flick the wrist" after releasing a jump shot. This puts rotation on the ball and gives the shot a nice, high arc.

Shooting the Ball

There are many different types of shots that can be used to put the ball in the hoop. The most common shots are jump shots and layups. A player takes a jump shot, or jumper, by

The Layup

To make a layup easier, use the backboard. Dribble the ball until you are about five feet from the basket. (You can dribble even closer when you are first learning this shot.) Pick up the ball in one hand and then take a step toward the basket. If you are shooting with your right hand, jump off your left foot. Kick your right knee to get maximum height on your jump. Aim your shot at the box behind the rim and try to bank the ball into the hoop. Keep practicing until you make your layup every time you shoot.

The reverse layup is a special kind of layup. For this shot, drive to the hoop as if taking a regular layup. But, instead of shooting from the normal side of the basket, dribble a few extra feet and pass under the hoop, turning around to shoot the ball from the reverse side. This shot is difficult to defend, since it is unexpected.

A layup is the easiest way to score when close to the basket. Practicing layups should be a regular part of your drills.

leaping in the air and releasing the shot at the highest point. Just about all outside shots are jump shots. Jump shots are effective because they can be released quickly, and when they are taken while running, they are very hard to block.

A layup, on the other hand, is a shot taken very close to the hoop. A layup is generally much easier to make than a jump shot.

A slam dunk, or jam, is a shot thrown straight down through the hoop. To make this shot, the player must be able to jump high in the air. Obviously, taller players have an advantage in making this shot.

A very effective shot that has fallen out of favor is the hook shot. For a hook shot, you turn to the side, extend your shooting arm high in the air, and release the ball one-handed. Kareem Abdul-Jabbar used his hook shot, nicknamed the sky hook, to score more points than any other player in NBA history.

Running Plays

Individual ball-handling skills and a good shooting touch are great to have, but basketball games are won and lost as a team. On offense, all five players must be involved to create good scoring chances. And on defense, all five players must work hard to help each other out and make it difficult for the other team to score.

Offensive Plays

Next time you watch a good team play offense, look at the action away from the ball. You will see that each player knows his or her role in the offense. There are hundreds of different offensive plays that teams will run, many of which involve all five players. But there are some very effective plays that require only two players. These include the pick and the give-and-go.

To set a pick, also called a screen, you stand still beside the opponent who is defending your teammate with the ball. Your teammate then dribbles so that he or she runs the defender into you. This often creates enough space for your teammate to attempt an uncontested shot. In a variation called the pick-and-roll, you set a pick and then turn ("roll") toward the basket. Turn quickly and use your backside to pin the defender you picked. Your teammate can then pass the ball back to you, and you'll often have an open shot at the basket.

29

Picking-and-Rolling into the Hall of Fame

For sixteen seasons, power forward Karl Malone and point guard John Stockton played together for the Utah Jazz. Over that time, their primary weapon was the pick-and-roll play. Using the pick-and-roll just about every time down the court, Malone became the NBA's second all-time career scoring leader. And Stockton, the player who passed the ball back to Malone, became the NBA's all-time career assist leader.

For a give-and-go, you simply pass the ball to a teammate ("give") and quickly break toward the basket ("go"). If your defender reacts slowly, your teammate can bounce-pass the ball back to you, and you'll have an open path to the basket.

Other offensive plays include the fast break, also called the running game, the high-post and low-post, the triangle, and motion offense. Different offensive tactics are used depending on the defense's strengths and weaknesses.

Defensive Plays

While it is critical to score points, a good defense is just as important as a good offense. Like offense, defense in basketball is a team concept that starts with strong individual skills. Being a good defender starts with pride and the right attitude. You have to dedicate yourself to the task and refuse to allow your opponents to score. Getting scored on should make you more

On defense, taller players use timing and jumping ability to block opponents' shots. This defender (*facing page, left*) helps his team by swatting away a shot close to the net.

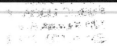

determined to stop your opponent the next time down the court. Even if your shot is not falling on the offensive end, you can always play fierce defense.

To make a steal without fouling, a good individual defender anticipates the play and then knocks the ball away without making contact with the ball handler. The defender may also make a steal by anticipating a pass. It is usually much easier to steal a pass than to take the ball from another player, so being able to see the entire floor and understand the other team's offense is a critical skill.

Shot blocking is another crucial defensive skill. This is an important part of a center's game. If a shot is on the way up, it is legal to knock it away. However, once the ball reaches the top of its arc, no player can touch it. Interfering with a ball in its downward flight is a violation called goaltending. The goaltending rule keeps tall players from standing in front of the basket and swatting away every shot.

Just like offenses, team defenses have their own setups. The most common is man-to-man defense, in which each defender guards one offensive player. In colleges and high school, your team might also use a zone defense, in which you guard an area of the court instead of another player. If a ball handler comes into your area, you play aggressive defense against him or her.

Defenses may also try a half-court or full-court press, strategies that keep the offense from getting the ball upcourt easily. Some presses call for defenders to trap, meaning they force the ball handler to the sideline and then double-team him or her in an attempt to force a turnover. Presses often confuse the offense and force turnovers from violations or errant passes. The best way to beat a full-court press is to run a fast break, with quick, accurate passing. Doing so gets the ball into the frontcourt before the defense can get in position to trap.

Rebounding

Rebounding, or getting possession of the ball after a missed shot, is a key to winning. Good rebounders don't mind getting under the basket and playing

Playing Defense

The most important thing to remember on defense is to stay relaxed. Bend at the knees and keep your weight forward. Keep your back straight and lean into a crouch, holding your head up straight. As the saying goes, "You play defense with your feet." If you are up on the balls of your feet, you can change directions quickly. But you have to use your hands, too. Keep your arms out away from your body and move your hands to block the passing lanes. Try to swipe the ball from below to avoid a foul.

When playing defense, be sure to look left and right to see if an opponent is moving in to set a pick. Don't focus too closely on the ball. Good ball handlers can easily beat you with a crossover dribble or a ball fake. Instead, try to focus on your opponent's waist. The waist has to move in the direction the player is going, so by watching it, you will not be fooled by the fakes a good player will try to use.

a little rough, if necessary. Height and strength are obviously advantages in being a good rebounder, but proper positioning is just as important.

On defense, getting good position is called boxing out. When a shot is taken, you should establish position between the basket and the player you are guarding. Then turn, so that you are facing the basket. It's important to maintain contact with the player you are boxing out, so remember to put your "butt in the gut" of your opponent. Keep your elbows out and hands up. Watch the flight of the ball, anticipating where it will bounce if it doesn't go in the hoop. If the shot rattles off the rim, explode toward the ball and grab it with both hands.

If you are a taller player and you get a rebound, hold the ball high above your head. This will prevent pesky smaller opponents with quick hands from taking the ball from you. After securing the ball, look to make an outlet pass to a guard running up the court. This may result in a fast-break opportunity.

Or, if you are a good ball handler, you can dribble the ball yourself to start the fast break. Quickly turn upcourt and use a power dribble to get clear of the pack.

Offensive players try to rebound, too. Getting an offensive rebound is crucial, since it gives your team another chance to score. If you are a taller player, try to go right back up with a shot, before the defense can get in good position. If you are a smaller player, it is usually best to take the ball back out toward half-court and set up an offensive play.

Even if you already knew everything you read in this chapter, it is a safe bet that there is still plenty more for you to learn. John Wooden, the most successful NCAA coach ever, once said, "It's what we learn after we know it all that really counts."

This player (*facing page*) does a good job of boxing out her opponent to get the rebound. Always go for a rebound using both hands, and grip the ball tightly when you get it.

CHAPTER FOUR

Getting on the Court

If you want to get out and play a game of basketball, where can you go? Fortunately, there are many ways you can play, whether on a school team, with other groups, or on your own.

Many middle schools have basketball programs for both boys and girls that allow you to play in organized games against other schools. Most high schools have basketball teams, too. At bigger schools, the tryouts can be very competitive, and not everyone makes the team. But if you just want to play for fun, you can see if your school offers intramural games. These are games between students who want to play without the structure and extensive practice the varsity teams require. Intramural teams typically have players of all skill levels.

Outside of school, in many communities you can sign up for

To play your best, basketball requires energy, athleticism, and a high level of physical fitness.

leagues at the YMCA and YWCA or other youth organization. These leagues often are broken down by age or skill level.

You could also attend one of the many basketball camps that are held around the country, usually during the summer. At camp, you'll live, eat, and breathe basketball for a week or two. These are great places to meet other players and learn good techniques from experienced coaches.

Stretching and Conditioning

No matter when or where you play, always make sure you have the right protective equipment. Boys should always wear an athletic supporter. Knee pads or elbow pads are also a good idea, especially if you are playing on an outdoor court. You may also want to wear a mouthpiece and sports goggles, if you wear glasses.

Stretching major muscles is an important part of game preparation. Always stretch before and after playing to

Take stretching seriously. Loosening up your muscles and limbering up your joints will help you avoid injury.

These players are performing passing drills in practice. Such drills help sharpen the skills you need to succeed during the game.

prevent cramps. Prior to stretching, warm up a little with a short jog. (Warm muscles are easier to stretch.) Start your stretches with the muscles in your lower back and legs. These are the biggest muscles in your body and the ones that get the hardest workout while playing. Stand with your legs apart and toes pointed outward. Then bend slowly and steadily several times over both knees and straight ahead.

To stretch your hamstrings, sit on the floor with your knees together and your legs straight, and try to touch your toes.

Other Basketball Games You Can Play

If you don't have enough players for a full game of basketball, you might try HORSE or Around the World. In HORSE, you take a shot from anywhere on the court. If you make it, the other players have to make the same exact shot. If another player fails to make the shot, he or she gets a letter: H-O-R-S and then E. Once you have HORSE, you are out of the game. The winner is the last player without HORSE.

In Around the World, each player has to make shots in order, from specific places on the court. You can't move on to the next shot until you make the one you are taking. Play usually starts with a layup from the right side, followed by shots from around the court, and ending with a layup from the left side. The first player to go "Around the World" wins.

Groin pulls can take a long time to heal, so stretch your groin muscles as well. For this, sit on the floor and bring your feet together, sole to sole. Then try touching your knees to the ground, gently pushing with your elbows to get a better stretch.

After stretching, do a more vigorous warm-up to get your body ready for the real action. Warm-ups do not have to be complicated—just jog around the gym, and then dribble the ball for several minutes. Use this time to get a sense of how your body is feeling. Before a team practice, your coach will probably run a series of drills, including wind sprints (running very quickly from one end of the gym to another) and shooting and rebounding drills.

To play your best, you need to be in good physical condition. This means exercising regularly, in addition to just playing the game. Running or jogging is an excellent way to build up stamina and get your legs in shape. Push-ups and pull-ups help build the upper body strength that can help you shoot and rebound more effectively. Light weight lifting may also help.

Improving Your Game: Skills and Drills

A game like Around the World (see sidebar on page 39) can help you practice your shot. To develop your ball-handling skills, dribble, dribble, and then dribble some more. Keep the ball low at all times, and remember to work on both hands.

To become a better passer, you don't even need another player. Tape three targets at different heights on a wall, and then try to hit them with chest passes and bounce passes. Once you can hit each one consistently, move back until you can hit the targets from twenty feet away or farther.

Don't overlook your defensive skills. You can improve your defensive quickness and stamina by slide-stepping from one end of the court to the other and back. For this, stand in the proper defensive position, and then move sideways, quickly sliding your feet without crossing your legs. If you are doing it correctly, you'll feel a good burn in your upper legs.

If you already play basketball, you know that it is a fun sport that's also good for your health. If you have never played, consider basketball as a great way to develop your physical skills and build friendships that can last your entire life. If you want to know why basketball is such a popular game worldwide, go hit the court and find out!

GLOSSARY

barnstorm To tour through rural districts, putting on exhibitions.

confined Restricted or held within a location.

detrimental Harmful or damaging.

double-team To guard a single player with two defenders.

dribble To bounce a basketball.

errant Straying out-of-bounds.

fast break An attempt to score quickly by running up the court before the other team can get into defensive position.

field goal A made basket.

jump shot A shot taken by jumping in the air and releasing the ball at the top of the leap.

lane The painted rectangle under the basket at either end of the court.

penetrate To drive past a defender and get near the basket with the ball.

raucous Boisterous and disorderly.

shrouded Hidden or concealed.

stamina Endurance or staying power.

traveling Taking more than one step with the ball without dribbling; a basketball violation that results in a turnover.

turnover Giving the other team possession of the ball.

vigorous Active or energetic.

FOR MORE INFORMATION

Amateur Athletic Union (AAU)
320 Quail Run South
Altus, OK 73521
(580) 482-3254
Web site: http://www.aaugirlsbasketball.org

National Basketball Association (NBA)
League Office
645 Fifth Avenue, 19th Floor
New York, NY 10022
Web site: http://www.nba.com

National Collegiate Athletic Association (NCAA)
700 West Washington Street
P.O. Box 6222
Indianapolis, IN 46206-6222
(317) 917-6222
Web site: http://www.ncaa.org

YMCA of the USA
101 North Wacker Drive
Chicago, IL 60606
(800) 872-9622
Web site: http://www.ymca.net

YWCA of the USA
1015 18th Street NW, Suite 1100
Washington, DC 20036

(202) 467-0801

Web site: http://www.ywca.org

Web Sites

Due to the changing nature of Internet links, Rosen Publishing has developed an online list of Web sites related to the subject of this book. This site is updated regularly. Please use this link to access the list:

http://www.rosenlinks.com/scc/bask

Frazier, Walt "Clyde," and Alex Sachare. *The Complete Idiot's Guide to Basketball*. Indianapolis, IN: Alpha Books, 1998.

Kolb, Joseph. *Get Fit Now for High School Basketball: Strength and Conditioning for Ultimate Performance on the Court*. Long Island City, NY: Hatherleigh Press, 2003.

Miller, Faye Young. *Winning Basketball for Girls*. New York, NY: Facts on File, 2002.

Naismith, James. *Basketball: Its Origin and Development*. Omaha, NE: University of Nebraska Press, 1996.

Sacharski, Eric, ed. *Blackboard Strategies: Over 200 Favorite Plays from Successful Coaches for Nearly Every Possible Situation*. Brookfield, WI: Lessiter Publications, 1999.

Stewart, Mark. *Basketball: A History of Hoops*. London, England: Franklin Watts, 1999.

Stewart, Wayne. *The Little Giant Book of Basketball Facts*. New York, NY: Sterling, 2005.

BIBLIOGRAPHY

Garfinkle, Howard. *Five-Star Basketball Drills*. New York, NY: McGraw-Hill, 1998.

Krause, Jerry. *Coaching Basketball*. New York, NY: McGraw-Hill, 2002.

NBA.com. "Official Rules of the National Basketball Association." Retrieved May 1, 2006 (http://www.nba.com/analysis/rules_index.html).

Wolff, Alexander. *100 Years of Hoops: A Fond Look Back at the Sport of Basketball*. New York, NY: Warner Books, 1997.

Wooden, John, and Steve Jamison. *Wooden on Leadership*. New York, NY: McGraw-Hill, 2005.

INDEX

About the Author

Fred Ramen is a writer who lives in New York City. A longtime sports fan, he has previously written about basketball in his biography of one of the game's all-time greats, Jerry West (also from Rosen Publishing).

Photo Credits

Cover (top) © Yellow Dog Productions/Getty Images; cover (left) pp. 14, 24, 27, 28, 34, 37 by Darryl Bautista © The Rosen Publishing Group and Darryl Bautista; cover (right, court), pp. 1, 10, 12 (bottom), 16, 17, 18, 20, 22, 23, 38 © Shutterstock; p. 3 © www.istockphoto.com/Dusty Cline; p. 4 Naismith Memorial Basketball Hall of Fame; p. 8 © Corbis; p. 9 Bob Cousy/NBA Photo Library/NBAE via Getty Images; p. 12 (top) © www.istockphoto.com/Todd Harrison; p. 15 © Daniel Lippitt/AFP/Getty Images; pp. 19, 25, 31, 36 © Getty Images; back cover (soccer ball) © www.istockphoto.com/Pekka Jaakkola; back cover (paintball gear) © www.istockphoto.com/Jason Maehl; back cover (football helmet) © www.istockphoto.com/Stefan Klein; back cover (football) © www.istockphoto.com/Buz Zoller; back cover (baseball gear) © www.istockphoto.com/Charles Silvey; back cover (basketball) © www.istockphoto.com/Dusty Cline.

Designer: Nelson Sá; **Editor:** Christopher Roberts